MW01042769

WE BOTH READ®

Parent's Introduction

Whether your child is a beginning reader, a reluctant reader, or an eager reader, this book offers a fun and easy way to encourage and help your child in reading.

Developed with reading education specialists, **We Both Read** books invite you and your child to take turns reading aloud. You read the left-hand pages of the book, and your child reads the right-hand pages—which have been written at one of six early reading levels. The result is a wonderful new reading experience and faster reading development!

You may find it helpful to read the entire book aloud yourself the first time, then invite your child to participate the second time. As you read, try to make the story come alive by reading with expression. This will help to model good fluency. It will also be helpful to stop at various points to discuss what you are reading. This will help increase your child's understanding of what is being read.

In some books, a few challenging words are introduced in the parent's text, distinguished with **bold** lettering. Pointing out and discussing these words can help to build your child's reading vocabulary. If your child is a beginning reader, it may be helpful to run a finger under the text as each of you reads. Please also notice that a "talking parent" ☺ icon precedes the parent's text, and a "talking child" ☺ icon precedes the child's text.

If your child struggles with a word, you can encourage "sounding it out," but keep in mind that not all words can be sounded out. Your child might pick up clues about a word from the picture, other words in the sentence, or any rhyming patterns. If your child struggles with a word for more than five seconds, it is usually best to simply say the word.

Most of all, remember to praise your child's efforts and keep the reading fun. After you have finished the book, ask a few questions and discuss what you have read together. Rereading this book multiple times may also be helpful for your child.

Try to keep the tips above in mind as you read together, but don't worry about doing everything right. Simply sharing the enjoyment of reading together will increase your child's reading skills and help to start your child off on a lifetime of reading enjoyment!

Dragons Do NOT Go to School!

We Both Read: Level PK-K
Guided Reading: Level A

Text Copyright © 2020 by D.J. Panec
Illustrations Copyright © 2020 by Andy Elkerton
All rights reserved

We Both Read® is a trademark of Treasure Bay, Inc.

Published by Treasure Bay, Inc.
P.O. Box 119
Novato, CA 94948 USA

Printed in Malaysia

Library of Congress Catalog Card Number: 2019947794

ISBN: 978-1-60115-362-3

Visit us online at:
TreasureBayBooks.com

PR-11-19

Dragons Do NOT
Go to School!

By D.J. Panec

Illustrated by Andy Elkerton

TREASURE BAY

On Saturday, Rex was wearing his big dragon wings and running as he looked up to the **sky**. He hadn't grown his real wings yet, and he loved imagining he was a giant dragon flying high in the . . .

. . . **sky**.

3

Later that day, his mother reminded him that he was starting **school** in two days.

Rex flapped his big dragon wings and said, "Dragons do NOT go to . . . .

. . . school."

"Dragons DO go to **school**," Rex's mother said. "That's where *little* dragons learn how to be *big* dragons. Don't you want to learn how to breathe fire and fly?"

"I do want to learn those things," Rex said. "But I do not want to go to . . .

6

". . . school."

Rex's mother looked at **him**. "Why don't you want to go to school?" she asked.

Rex looked at the floor. "Because I don't know anyone there. What if no one wants to be my friend or play with me?"

Rex's mom told **him** she was sure that he would make a new friend who would play with . . .

. . . **him.**

Rex looked over at his **wings**. "Well," he said, "if I'm going to learn to fly at school, I should wear my big dragon . . .

. . . wings."

Rex's mother said she would talk with his **teacher** and see if he could wear the wings at least for the first day.

So Monday morning Rex and his mother went to school, where they met Rex's new . . .

. . . teacher.

Rex's teacher smiled and said he could wear the wings—but just for today. Then Rex gave his mom a hug goodbye and waved as she left the classroom.

"What's on your back?" asked a voice behind him. Rex turned and saw a dragon with purple spots, another with two green **horns**, and another with one blue . . .

. . . horn.

 **Rex** popped out his big dragon wings.

"Wow! Those are really cool wings!" said the dragon with the blue horn.

Rex smiled. "My grandpa and I made them," said . . .

. . . Rex.

"Those aren't real wings," said the dragon with green horns. "Those are pretend wings."

"I don't think you're allowed to wear things like that in school," said the dragon with purple . . .

. . . spots.

Rex didn't know what to say. He looked around for his mom and then remembered she had already left.

Rex's teacher clapped her hands and asked all the young dragons to take a seat on a big soft . . .

. . . rug.

That morning Rex learned some cool things about weather. He learned dragons can fly in any kind of weather—snow, fog, and even thunderstorms! He even got to **play** a drum that sounded like thunder.

Then the teacher said it was time for recess. It was time to go outside to . . .

 . . . **play.**

Rex wanted to join the dragons that were playing together outside, but he wasn't sure if they would let him. Then the dragon with the blue horn ran up to him and said, "I like that your wings are so **big**."

Rex grinned. "My grandpa wanted to make them small, but I wanted them to be really . . .

. . . big."

"My name is Kris," said the **dragon** with the blue horn.

"And I'm Rex," said Rex.

"I can breathe fire," said Kris. "I can breathe fire just like all the big . . .

. . . dragons."

"Can you really breathe **fire**?" Rex asked.

Kris turned to the side. Suddenly, Kris's mouth seemed to erupt with flames of . . .

. . . fire.

"That's not real fire!" said the dragon with green horns. "That's just a fan and some silly streamers."

"I don't think they allow things like that at school," said the dragon with purple . . .

. . . spots.

Rex looked at Kris, who didn't seem to know what to say.

Then, Rex stepped forward and popped out his wings. He took a big breath and said, "Well, I think Kris is the most amazing fire-breathing dragon I have ever . . .

. . . met!"

Kris and Rex ran all over the playground. Rex flew with his giant wings and Kris blew constant streams of fire. They didn't want to stop playing when they heard the ringing of the . . .

. . . bell.

That afternoon Rex told his mother everything he learned about weather. He told her that what he learned was going to help him fly better when he grew . . .

. . . up.

He also told her about his new friend, **Kris**. He pointed up to the sky and said that someday he was going to fly high above the clouds together with . . .

. . . Kris.

His mother asked if he would like to go to
school tomorrow, even without his big **dragon
wings**.

"Well," Rex said, "when I play with Kris, I
can always imagine I'm wearing my big . . .

. . . dragon wings."

 "I want to go **to school**," he said. "I want to learn to fly for real. Besides, my friend, Kris, goes **to school**—and you know, Mom, dragons always go . . .

. . . to school."

If you liked **Dragons Do NOT Go to School!,** here are some
other We Both Read® books you are sure to enjoy!

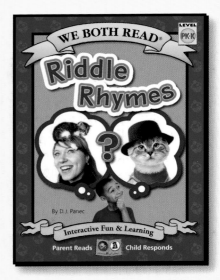

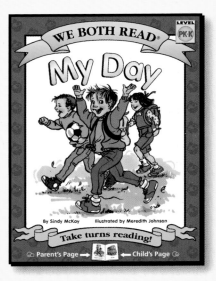

You can see all the We Both Read books that are available
at WeBothRead.com.